MARC BROWN

ARTHUR,
CLEAN YOUR ROOM!

A RED FOX BOOK

Published by Random House Children's Books 20 Vauxhall Bridge

A division of The Random House Group Ltd London Melbour

Johannesburg and agencies throughout the world

Copyright © 1999 Marc Brown

1 3 5 7 9 10 8 6 4 2

First published in the United States of America by Random House Inc., New York and
simultaneously in Canada by Random House of Canada Limited, Toronto 1999

First published in Great Britain by Red Fox 2000

Printed in Hong Kong by Midas Printing Limited

THE RANDOM HOUSE GROUP Limited Reg. No. 954009

ISBN 0 09 940797 3

D0510038

Red Fox

"Mom, I can't find
my Bionic Bunny,"
said Arthur.
"No wonder," Arthur's mother said.
"Look at all this junk!"

"It's not junk," said Arthur.
"It IS junk," she said,
"and I want you to get rid of it –
NOW!"

"But how can I get rid of it?"
said Arthur.
"Sell it," said D.W.
"You can make lots of money."

"Have a garage sale," said Mother.
"And have it today."

D.W. helped Arthur carry
boxes of junk outside.
"I've always liked
your Jolly Jingle Maker,"
said D.W. "Can I have it?"
"I'm selling it," said Arthur.

GARAGE
SALE
TODAY

ROCKS

Buster was the first one there.
"I can't believe you're selling
this Bionic Bunny Jet Fighter,"
he said. "I don't have a dollar,
but I'll trade you my
Bionic Bunny Spy Glasses."

"Your Bionic Bunny Spy Glasses!"
said Arthur. "OK, great trade!"
Buster ran to his house
to get them.

Then Francine came along with
a cart filled with comics.
"My mom is making me get rid
of these," she said sadly.
"Brilliant! Cool Cat comics!"
said Arthur.
"Wow!" said Francine.
"Table football!"
"Almost new," said Arthur.
"I'll trade it for your comics."
"All right!" said Francine.

News spread, and Arthur's friends
all came with things to trade.
"Binky, that is so cool,"
said Arthur. "What is it?"
"My punching bag," said Binky.
"I want to trade it
for your Sailor Sam Ship."
"Good deal!" said Arthur.

Muffy showed up next.
"You've always liked
my clubhouse flag,"
she said. "Want to trade?"
"Sure," said Arthur.
"Is this cute waistcoat
really yours, Arthur?"
she giggled.
"It's yours now," he said.
"It's never been worn."

The Brain came with a radio.

"It needs a little work," he said.

"I'll trade you my elephant mask,"
said Sue Ellen.

Prunella traded
her rock star poster.

Fern had a typewriter
that Arthur really liked.

Arthur was happy.

His old stuff was gone.

D.W. ran to the garage.

"You didn't sell your

Jolly Jingle Maker," she said.

"But I got rid of all my other

old stuff," said Arthur.

"I'll count your money,"
said D.W.
"Well," he said,
"I didn't really get money…"

"But I got all this great new stuff."

"If Mom sees this," said D.W.,
"you're in big trouble."
"You're right," he said,
"but what am I going to do?"
"I have a plan,"
whispered D.W.

Later that day, Arthur's mother
went to check his room.
Arthur followed her up the stairs.
He crossed his fingers
and held his breath.

"Good job, Arthur," she said.
"You got rid of all your junk."
Just then they heard a big
CRASH!
They ran to D.W.'s room.

Junk was everywhere.

"Dora Winifred!" shouted Mother.

"What is this mess?"

"It's not a mess," said D.W.

"It's business.

Arthur is paying me rent.

And he owes me a dollar."

"I don't have a dollar," said
Arthur. "How about a trade?"